Counting
Belize
Frogs and Toads

Caye to Learning Series:

In this series of pre-school books, I have presented basic concepts using Jim Beveridge's wildlife photographs which were all taken in Belize. By using local wildlife photos, Belizean children will learn about their natural heritage. These books are designed to help the parent/guardian/educator to teach young children about numbers, letters, colors, shapes, sizes and spatial relationships in a fun and interactive method enjoyable to the child and the adult.

Books in the Caye to Learning Series

Counting Belize Frogs and Toads
Belize Living Alphabet
Birding in Belize with Colours
Beautiful Belize Reef

Counting
Belize
Frogs and Toads

Dorothy Beveridge
Photographs by Jim Beveridge

Caye to Learning Series 1

Producciones de la Hamaca

Caye Caulker, BELIZE

2012

Published by *Producciones de la Hamaca*
Caye Caulker, BELIZE
<producciones-hamaca.com>

ISBN: 978-976-8142-47-4 (print edition)
ISBN: 978-976-8142-74-0 (e-book edition)

Counting Belize Frogs and Toads is the 1st in the *Caye to Learning Series*
ISBN: 978-976-8142-46-7

Producciones de la Hamaca is dedicated to:
- Celebration and documentation of Belize's rich, diverse cultural heritage,
- Protection and sustainable use of Belize's remarkable natural resources,
- Inspired, creative expression of Belize's spiritual depth.

In the Belize Rainforest, many frogs and toads are hidden. With your help, let's find and count them.

One marine toad hopping.

Two pepper tree frogs visiting.

3 three

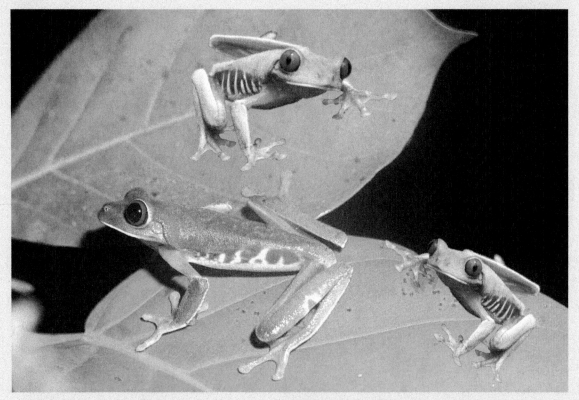

Three red-eyed tree frogs sitting.

4

four

Four Mexican tree frogs croaking.

5   **five**

Five gulf coast toads hopping.

6
six

Six red-eyed tree frogs sleeping.

7
seven

Seven bromeliad tree frogs on a leaf.

eight

Eight hour glass frogs resting and croaking.

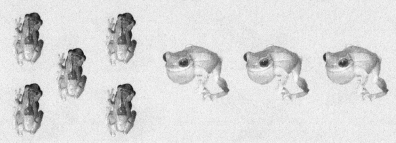

9   nine

Nine vaillant frogs swimming.

10 ten

Ten barking tree frogs waiting.

Count the tree frogs.

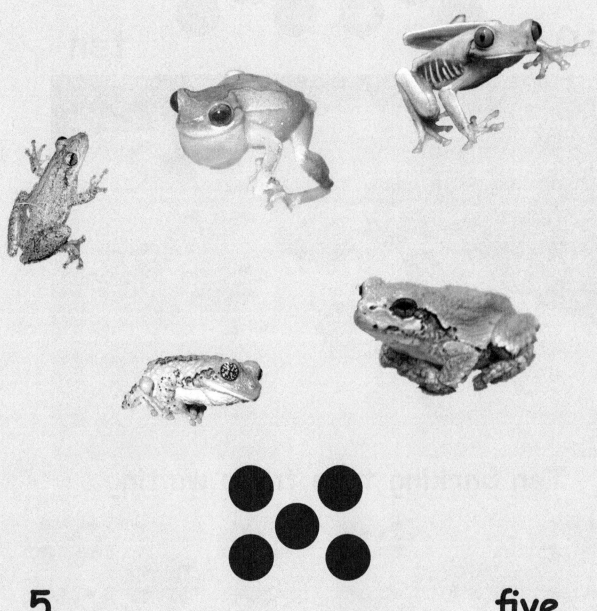

5   five

Count the toads.

2   two

Count the frogs and toads.

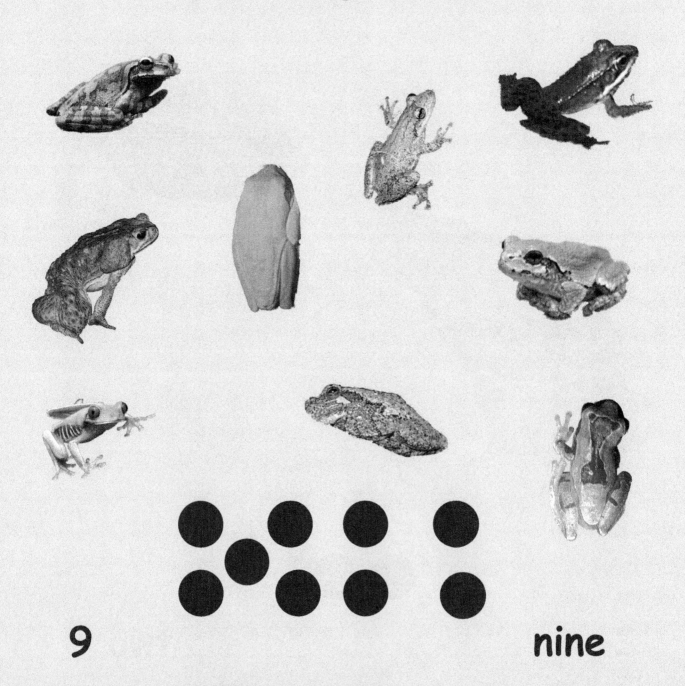

9   nine

Find and count the frogs.

4   four

Mexican tree frogs singing in a lagoon.

How many frogs can you count?

Red-eyed Tree frogs lay eggs on leaves. These eggs grow into tadpoles.

How many tadpoles can you count?
How many eggs can you count?

In the Belize Rainforest, many frogs and toads are hidden. With your help, let's find and count them.

You have been counting frogs and toads.

Now look around you.

What do you see that you can count?

So begin now and count.

1, 2, 3, 4, 5, 6, 7, 8, 9, 10

Dorothy Beveridge was born and raised in North Carolina, USA. She earned her BA in Early Childhood Education and taught in pre-schools and primary schools. After moving to Belize, she volunteered with Belize Audubon Society and Belize Tourism Industry Association doing enviromental education. She has been writing children's books for her young relatives and friends' children for many years. Using her husband's wildlife photographs, she has written a children's series, *Caye to Learning*.

Jim Beveridge was born and raised in Scotland. He has traveled extensively in Europe and the Americas. He has worked in a variety of fields as a carpenter, salvage diver, master plumber, SCUBA dive master, and underwater and wildlife photographer. His photos have been published in international journals and books, such as, *Nature Conservancy Magazine, Watching Wildlife: Central America, The Rough Guide to Belize, Wanted Alive/Fragile Frogs, Cultures of the World: Belize, Tree Frog, Medicines from Nature*, as well as other books, textbooks, magazines, and calendars. Articles written and illustrated by Jim have been published in *Cockscomb Basin Wildlife Sanctuary, Aqua Geõgraphia, Belize Audubon Society Newsletter*, and other publications. In 2012 his book, *Wildlife-Wild Places*, was published.